CHURCH~ LIBRARY
020 8359 3800

KU-071-647

Please return/renew this item by the
last date shown to avoid a charge.
Books may also be renewed by phone
and Internet. May not be renewed if
required by another reader.

www.libraries.barnet.gov.uk

BARNET
LONDON BOROUGH

THE
GREAT
TELEPHONE
MIX-UP

THE GREAT TELEPHONE MIX-UP

SALLY NICHOLLS

Illustrated by
Sheena Dempsey

Barrington Stoke

First published in 2018 in Great Britain by
Barrington Stoke Ltd
18 Walker Street, Edinburgh, EH3 7LP

www.barringtonstoke.co.uk

Text © 2018 Sally Nicholls
Illustrations © 2018 Sheena Dempsey

A CIP catalogue record for this book is available
from the British Library upon request

ISBN: 978-1-78112-735-3

Printed in China by Leo

This book is in a super readable format for young readers
beginning their independent reading journey.

*To the village of Cliffords Mesne,
whose real-life telephone mix-up made
me want to write this story.*

CONTENTS

CHAPTER 1

The Telephone Line

Once, there was a village.

In the village, there was a storm.

The rain rained.

The wind blew.

Thunder rumbled.

And lightning STRUCK!

It struck a big old tree on the edge of the village.

The tree fell onto the telephone wire.

And all the telephones in the village went DEAD.

The next morning, the villagers woke up and none of their telephones worked.

Margaret was very cross. Margaret was trying to organise a village May Fair, a pack of cub scouts, a choir, a cinema club and the local Women's Institute.

Margaret got lots of very important phone calls every day. There wasn't any mobile signal in the village, so she needed her home phone – all the time!

Will was glad his mum didn't have a telephone that day. People mostly rang his mum to be cross about what Will had been up to.

Will thought it was very nice not to have the phone ringing all the time.

So did Will's mum.

Jai was worried about not having a phone. His friend Aditi might ring and not be able to talk to him. What if she thought he was ignoring her?

Jean was old and not very good at walking. She lived all alone with her little cat, Charlie. She was scared about not having a phone. What if she needed help? How would she let anybody know?

Arthur didn't care about the telephone. Nobody ever rang him anyway. He went to ride his bike in the garden of his new house, and let his

mum and dad worry about it. Arthur
and his mum and dad had just moved
to the village, so they were very busy
right now.

"What a mess!" Margaret said. "Someone needs to sort this out. And that someone is me."

Margaret got into her car and drove to town. There was mobile-phone signal in town.

She called the telephone company on her mobile phone.

"All of our telephones are broken!" she said. "Please send someone to fix them right away!"

So the telephone company did.

Two people came and put the telephone pole back up. They took the broken wires and they fixed them together again.

But something went wrong.

Some of the wires got put together in the wrong way.

And the next day, when everyone in the village woke up ...

... there was trouble.

CHAPTER 2

Will's Mum Is Confused

The next day, Will's mum was making breakfast. The telephone rang.

"Hello?" Will's mum said.

"Hello!" a man said. "Where would you like your bouncy castle?"

"My bouncy castle?" Will's mum said. She didn't know what the man was talking about. "What bouncy castle?"

"Well, that's up to you," the man said. "Would you like our Small Bouncy Castle, our Medium Bouncy Castle, or our Super-Dooper Extra-Bouncy Bouncy Castle With Added Turrets?"

"I don't want a bouncy castle at all," Will's mum said. "Thank you very much."

And she put the phone down.

She was filling the tea-pot when the telephone rang again.

"Hello?" she said.

"Best hellos!" a cheerful voice said. "Good news! I've got two donkeys who can give donkey-rides to the children!"

"Oh," Will's mum said. "Er. Good."

"Isn't it?" the cheerful voice said. "Can you find someone to take the money for the donkey-rides? And the donkeys will need hay and water. Can you sort that out?"

"Um," said Will's mum. "Well. I think you might have got the wrong –"

"Thanks a lot!" the cheerful person said. "Toodle-doo!"

'Huh,' Will's mum thought. She felt a bit worried.

Was someone going to come and deliver a bouncy castle and two donkeys to her house?

She and Will had almost finished their breakfast when the phone rang again.

'Oh, bother!' she thought and stomped over to answer it.

"What?" she said.

"Hello!" said the lady on the other end. "I'm ringing about the brass band –"

"What brass band?" said Will's mum. "I don't want a brass band."

"Are you sure?" the lady said. "They WILL be disappointed. They've been practising all year."

"What would I do with a brass band?" Will's mum said. "I hate brass bands! I like donkeys, but I don't want to feed them, and I haven't got space in my garden for a bouncy castle. Who are you all, and why do you keep ringing me?"

There was a pause. Then the lady said, "Isn't this Margaret?"

"No!" Will's mum said. "It is not!"

"Oh," the lady said. "Sorry about that!"

And she put the phone down.

CHAPTER 3

Jai Is Shouted at and Jean Is Surprised

Jai had a very nice day. He spent it climbing up the side of a mountain. (Jai ran a rock-climbing club.)

When he got home, the phone was ringing.

"Hello?" he said. "Aditi, is that you?"

"No, it is not!" an angry woman said. "It's Will's teacher! Is Will's mum there?"

"No, she isn't," said Jai.

"Well, you tell her from me," the teacher said, "Will's done it again!"

"I think you've got the wrong number," said Jai, and he put the phone down.

It started to ring again.

"Hello?" said Jai.

"Hello!" an angry man said. "Do you know what your son's just done? He's climbed on top of my roof and tipped red paint down my chimney pot!"

"Oh," said Jai. He wanted to giggle. "Why did he do that?"

"Because I told him off for playing football on the green," the voice said.

"But kids are allowed to play football on the green," said Jai.

There was pause. Then,

"Are you Will's mum?" the voice said.

"No! Of course I'm not," said Jai.

The person at the other end of the phone rang off.

'Heavens above,' Jai thought.

Jean was very pleased when her telephone rang. 'Oh, good!' she thought. 'It's working again!'

"Hello?" she said.

"Hello," said a young woman in a nice voice. "Is Jai there, please? It's Aditi."

"No he isn't, dear," Jean said. "He doesn't live here, I'm afraid."

"Oh!" said the woman called Aditi.

She rang off. A few seconds later, the telephone rang again.

"Hello?"

"Me again, I'm afraid," said Aditi. "Is there something wrong with the telephone line?"

"I don't know, dear," said Jean. "I suppose there must be."

CHAPTER 4

Arthur Is Helpful and Margaret Is Confused

Arthur was playing with his farm animals. The telephone rang.

"Hello?" he said.

"Hello," said a voice. "Is Jean Johnson there, please?"

"No," Arthur said. "She doesn't live here."

"Oh," the voice said. "Thank you."

"You're welcome," Arthur said, and he put down the phone.

It started to ring again.

"Hello?" Arthur said.

"Hello," the voice said. "It's you again."

"Yes," Arthur said. "Can I give Jean a message? She lives at the end of our road."

"All right," said the voice. "That's kind. Could you tell Jean we have a place for her at Sunny Side Old People's Home, please?"

"No problem," Arthur said, and he went back to his farm animals.

Margaret was very worried. She hadn't had any phone calls all day! What was happening?

'Huh,' she thought. 'That stupid telephone company!'

Margaret lifted her phone. It sounded like it was working. She called the telephone company.

"Have you fixed my telephone line?" she demanded.

"I don't know," a woman's voice said. "Why don't you try to ring someone?"

"I am!" Margaret said. "I'm ringing you!"

"Oh," said the voice. "So you are. Then yes. We have fixed it."

"Then why has nobody called me?" said Margaret. "I haven't had a single phone call all day!"

And so the villagers spent all day going from house to house taking messages to one another. Before long they worked out what had happened. The phone lines had got in a muddle! Everyone's telephone number went to a different house!

"This is a disaster!" Margaret said. "I shall tell the telephone company to fix it right away!"

"Oh well," Jai said. "It could be worse. We'll just have to be extra-helpful until the muddle is fixed."

"I should hope so too!" Margaret said.

CHAPTER 5

Will's Mum Gets Lots of Phone Calls

Margaret had a very quiet week.

On Monday, Arthur's granny in Aberdeen rang up.

"WHO do you want to talk to?" Margaret said. She had never met Arthur's family.

"They've just moved to your village," Arthur's granny said, and she gave Margaret their address.

"Oh!" Margaret said.

On Thursday, Arthur's mum's friend in Cardiff called.

And that was it.

Nobody phoned about Cubs or Scouts.

Or the Women's Institute.

Or the cinema club.

Or the May Fair.

Hardly anyone rang Arthur's mum and dad, so Margaret's phone hardly rang all week. It was very peaceful.

'Of course,' Margaret thought. 'Arthur and his family have only just moved here. They probably don't know many people.'

And then she thought, 'I wonder if they're lonely?'

Will's mum, on the other hand, had a lot of phone calls.

Phone calls about the Cubs.

Phone calls about the Women's Institute.

Phone calls about the cinema club.

And lots and lots of phone calls about the May Fair.

The people ringing her up said,

"Have you found someone to run the tombola?"

"Have you found something for the children to do?"

"Can you be there early to set up?"

Will's mum wrote all the messages down, and every day she took them round to Margaret. Margaret didn't look very happy.

'Poor Margaret,' Will's mum thought. 'What a lot of work she has!'

And then she thought, 'I wonder why nobody helps her?'

Jai also got a lot of phone calls.

First Will's teacher rang to say Will was sitting at the top of the big tree in the playground and wouldn't come down.

Then Margaret rang to say Will had written rude words on the roof of the Scout Hut.

Then the vicar rang to say Will had climbed up the church tower.

Jai went to tell Will's mum.

"Oh dear!" Will's mum said with a big sigh. Then she gave Jai a cup of tea and a slice of cake.

"Sorry, Mum," Will said. "But I DID get to the top of the tower! Are you impressed?"

"No, I am not!" said his mum.

"I am," said Jai. And he was.

CHAPTER 6

Jean Makes a Friend

Jean got another phone call from Aditi.

"Hello," Jean said. "I'm afraid it's not Jai. It's me again." And she told Aditi all about the great telephone mix-up.

"How interesting for you all," Aditi said. "You'll find out everyone's secrets!"

"I can give Jai a message if you like," Jean said. "He lives next door to the woman who delivers my Meals on Wheels."

"All right," said Aditi. "Can you tell him to call Aditi, please?"

"Of course," said Jean. "How do you know Jai? I do like him."

"Do you?" Aditi said. "So do I. I used to go rock-climbing with him. But then I hurt my legs and had to stop."

"Oh, dear!" Jean said.

"Yes," Aditi said. "But I've found some special harnesses to help me climb. We're going to buy some for the rock-climbing club."

"How exciting!" Jean said. "Maybe I could have a go."

"Of course you could!" Aditi said. "What a brilliant idea."

After that, Aditi rang Jean quite a lot. They talked about all sorts of things.

Jai also came round a lot to see if Jean had any messages. He brought her some of Will's mum's cake.

"You could just ring Aditi yourself, you know," said Jean.

Jai went pink.

"Oh yes," he said. "Yes. I could do that. But – well – I don't – I mean …"

"Because you're shy," said Jean.

And Jai nodded.

"I'm not normally a shy person," he said. "But Aditi ... well. Aditi's special. She always makes me feel shy."

CHAPTER 7

Arthur Has an Idea

Arthur's family liked getting Jean's phone calls. Every time they got a phone call, they went round to see her. They heard all about the old people's home Jean was going to move to. They met Charlie, Jean's cat. Arthur loved Charlie. He was warm and old and soft and gentle. He didn't want to chase mice or play with balls of wool. He liked to lie on Arthur's lap and be stroked. His fur was the softest thing Arthur had ever felt.

"Are you sad about going to live in a home?" Arthur said to Jean.

"Oh no," Jean said. "I'm too old to live here now. It will be nice not to be worried all the time. They have a lovely big garden. And trips to the seaside."

But she sighed. She didn't look happy.

"You ARE sad," said Arthur. "Why are you sad?"

But Jean wouldn't say.

The phone was ringing when Arthur got home from school. He picked it up.

"Hello?" he said.

"Hello," a lady said. "Are you the family who gets Jean Johnson's phone calls?"

"That's us," said Arthur.

"Well," the lady said in a kind voice. "Could you tell Jean that we're sorry, but she CAN'T have Charlie in our old people's home?"

"Oh," Arthur said.

"I know," the kind lady said. "I wish she could. But I'm sure she'll find somebody to look after him."

Arthur put down the phone. So that
was why Jean was so sad!

Arthur didn't think it would be easy
to find someone to look after Charlie.
He was a very old cat, and he was smelly
and nearly blind.

But Jean loved him.

'And,' Arthur thought, 'so do I.'

Arthur and his mum and dad went to see Jean. She was in her chair by the window with Charlie on her lap. Arthur's mum came and held her hand.

"We've just had a phone call," she said. "The old people's home say they can't look after Charlie. I'm so sorry."

Jean sighed. A tear rolled out of her eye.

"Oh dear, oh dear," she said. "Poor Charlie. Who will take care of him now?"

"We will," Arthur said. "If you'll let us. We'll bring him to visit you. Please let us. We'd love to look after Charlie."

CHAPTER 8

Margaret Is Busy

Arthur and his mum and dad talked about Charlie all the way home.

"I will miss Jean," Arthur's mum said. "It's been nice to have a friend in the village."

When they got home, Margaret was standing on their doorstep.

"Hello," Arthur's mum said. "Is there a phone message for us?"

"No," Margaret said. "Doesn't it make you sad?" she said. "That no one ever phones you?"

"Well ..." Arthur's dad said. "We're new here. We don't know anybody yet."

"Most of our old friends email us," said Arthur's mum.

"But you could join things!" said Margaret. "There are lots of things to join! The cinema club! The Sunday School!"

"We don't really go to church," Arthur's dad said.

"The cub pack!"

"Ooh!" Arthur said. "Can I join the cubs, Mum?"

"The choir!" Margaret went on.

"Ooh," Arthur's mum said. "I love singing!"

"There are lots of nice people in the choir," said Margaret. "I'll send some round to say hello."

"Oh," Arthur's mum said. And "Well," and "Um," and "I mean to say ..."

Then – "Thank you very much," she said. "That would be lovely."

Will's mum and Jai had another cup of tea and another slice of cake and talked about Margaret.

"I do feel sorry for her," Will's mum said. "People are always ringing her up with more jobs and she never says 'No' to them. She needs help, that's what she needs."

"What sort of help?" said Jai.

"Well," Will's mum said. "If somebody would organise a cake stall, that would help. She can't find anyone to do that."

"You could do that," Jai said.

Will's mum looked surprised. Then she said, "I suppose I could!"

"And she needs someone to organise something for the children. I don't know what."

"How about a climbing wall?" Jai said. "I could do that."

"And she needs someone to help her set up all the stalls. We could all do that, couldn't we? Me and you and Will. And Will could run the tombola – he'd like that. And – who could we ask to take money for the donkey-rides?"

"My friend Aditi!" Jai said. "She'd love that." He beamed at Will's mum.

"Aren't we clever?" he said.

"We're brilliant," Will's mum said.

CHAPTER 9

Jai Also Has an Idea

All the way home, Jai thought about how they'd solved Margaret's problem. And how much he liked Will and his mum.

'I wish I could help Will,' he thought.

Then he had an idea.

He turned round and went back to Will's house.

"Will!" Jai said. "You like to climb things! How would you like to come rock-climbing on Saturday?"

"Really?" Will said.

"Yes," Jai said. "You can come every Saturday if you want. But you have to stop climbing with no ropes. It's stupid and dangerous. And we don't let stupid people join our rock-climbing club."

Will thought about it. Then he grinned.

"All right," he said. "Cool!"

After he saw Will, Jai went to Jean's house. Aditi answered the door.

"Hello!" Jai said, very surprised. "What are you doing here?"

"I came to say 'thank you' to Jean for passing on my messages," Aditi said.

Jean came out of the kitchen.

"There you are!" she said. "I've just met your lovely girlfriend! You ARE lucky!"

"Oh!" said Aditi, and,

"Oh!" said Jai.

"We're not –" Aditi said.

"She isn't –" Jai said.

"She isn't?" Jean said. "Why ever not?"

"Well –" Aditi said. And she blushed. "He doesn't –"

"I don't?" Jai said. "She doesn't –"

"Oh, for goodness sake!" Jean said. "She thinks you're wonderful! Anyone can see that!"

Jai went pink.

"Do you?" he said.

"Of course she does!" said Jean. "And he thinks you're wonderful," she said to Aditi. "He's ALWAYS asking if you've phoned!"

"Are you?" Aditi said.

"Yes," said Jean. "So stop being so silly, both of you."

Aditi and Jai looked at each other. Then they both started to laugh.

CHAPTER 10

The Village May Fair

The May Fair was the best May Fair the village had ever had.

Aditi and Jai were very happy.

"Didn't you know I liked you?" said Jai.

"No," said Aditi. "I thought you were just being nice. Didn't you know I liked you?"

Will was very happy. He ran the tombola stall, and he helped Jai with the climbing wall, and everyone said how good he was at climbing. He helped Jean climb half way up using Aditi's special harness, and he taught the vicar how to abseil.

"Isn't Will clever?" everyone said. Which made Will's mum very happy too.

Arthur was happy because Charlie was going to be his cat. His mum and dad were happy because they'd made some new friends in the village. And joined the cinema club and the choir.

Jean was happy because Charlie was happy.

"We'll come and visit you all the time!" Arthur said.

And Margaret was happy because the May Fair was a success.

At the end of the May Fair, Margaret made a speech.

"I have some very good news," she said. "I had a call from the telephone company this morning. All our telephones have been fixed!"

Everyone cheered.

"Thank heavens for that!" Will's mum said.

"I don't know," said Jai. "I've rather enjoyed it. I think I'm a bit sad that our great telephone mix-up is over."

Our books are tested
for children and young people by
children and young people.

Thanks to everyone who consulted on
a manuscript for their time and effort in
helping us to make our books better
for our readers.